MAGIC BEACH

Copyright © 2005 by the Estate of Ruth Krauss
Appreciation copyright © 2005 by Maurice Sendak
Afterword copyright © 2005 by Philip Nel

The publisher gratefully acknowledges the
cooperation of the Smithsonian Institution.

Designed by Rob Day
All rights reserved
Printed in China
First edition

LIBRARY OF CONGRESS CATALOGING-IN-PUBLICATION DATA
Johnson, Crockett, 1906–1975
Magic beach / by Crockett Johnson.—1st ed.
p. cm.
Originally published with illustrations by Betty
Fraser in 1965 under the title: Castles in the sand.
Summary: Two children find themselves in a story
when they write words in the sand on the beach,
and whatever they have written appears when the
waves wash the words away.
ISBN 1-932425-27-6 (alk. paper)
[1. Fantasy.] I. Johnson, Crockett, 1906–1975, Castles in the sand. II. Title.
PZ7.J63162Mag 2005
[E]–dc22
2005012054

▌ FRONT STREET

An Imprint of Boyds Mills Press, Inc.
A Highlights Company

MAGIC
BEACH

CROCKETT JOHNSON

With an Appreciation by *Maurice Sendak*

and an Afterword by *Philip Nel*

FRONT STREET   Asheville, North Carolina

"I wouldn't mind if we were in a story," said Ann. "Because people in stories don't go around all day looking for an old shell. Interesting things happen."

"Nothing really happens in a story," said Ben. "Stories are just words. And words are just letters. And letters are just different kinds of marks."

WHAT ARE THESE BRAVE, new, Beckett-like kids doing in a children's book written in the 1960s? They're very smart and have no difficulty living in a world that contains both the real and the unreal—a literary world, a world denied the many grownups who have lost the power to imagine and to believe in that imagining. Ann and Ben belong, of course, to Crockett Johnson, the extraordinary creator of Barnaby and of the very famous Harold with his purple crayon, smarty-pants kids who helped change the stuffy old face of children's book publishing. As far as these kids are concerned, we are all—grownups and children—welcome to live in any way we like, in the real and the unreal at the same time.

In *Magic Beach* there is the fresh, modern tempo and the sly nuttiness that elevated all the books by Crockett Johnson and Ruth Krauss, his brilliant wife and perfect partner in ingenious practical nonsense. I was the lucky Brooklyn kid, rough-edged and totally untrained, who met up with this pair in the early '50s. They took a fancy to me and, in their typically unorthodox way, let me hang around—practically live with them—in their old-fashioned roomy Connecticut house near a river. I illustrated nine of Ruth's astonishing books and was there for the creation of Harold, and Crockett Johnson was always there for me. I listened and learned.

Crockett and Ruth provided amazing sweet pleasure for generations of new children living in a bewildering, war-shocked, weary world: simple-seeming, quick-flashing prose and poetry; the precise mimicking of children's strange ways and the skillful evoking of their ego-centered universe; the musings, cockeyed humor, and dark fantasies of the child's soul; and the love, trust, and perfect freedom to let kids be who they were in a world created just for them. And in so simple and modest a form! Jane Austen, when lavishly praised for her great novels, claimed to have painted with only the tiniest brush on the smallest piece of ivory. Crockett and Ruth show that same touching honesty and humility in their work. But they are huge in their sharp wit, their wacky, fruitcake humor, their deep and abounding concern. What is universally clear is their shared love for kids, their intense curiosity as to what a kid is. There has never been another pair like Crockett and Ruth, before or after.

A serious/comic reflection of the world that was, *Magic Beach* was way ahead of its time, so much so that it was not accepted for publication as Crockett conceived it—he was not the illustrator of the 1965 edition of the story, published under the title *Castles in the Sand*. It is nothing less than a miracle that the original dummy with the complete manuscript and his sketches should ever have reappeared and been resurrected. Crockett did not finish the diamond-in-the-rough drawings you'll see here, and even if he had, he might not have approved them. He was a bit rueful about his book illustrations; they all looked the same, he thought. To my mind, these drawings show his healthy artistic impulse and epitomize his tried-and-true genius. They speak for him, and we love and trust them for their endearing familiarity. The sketches were intended only to show his editor the direction he meant to go in, but, for me, they are as finished as any illustrations he ever did. Only better.

"I'm tired," said Ann. "We should have stayed at the cottage and read a story."

"It's more fun to do something yourself instead of reading about it," said Ben.

"I wouldn't mind if we were in a story,"
said Ann. "Because people in stories
don't go around all day looking for an
old shell. Interesting things happen."

"Nothing really happens in a story,"
said Ben. "Stories are just words. And
words are just letters. And letters are
just different kinds of marks."

He begin to make marks in the sand.

"I wish I had some bread and jam,"
said Ann. "I'm hungry."

Ben frowned.

"And you're hungry, too," said Ann.
"You spelled out JAM."

Water from a gently breaking wave
flooded the sand, then slid back.

The marks were gone.

And at the edge of the wet sand
a silver dish appeared, full of jam.

Ben and Ann stared at it.

Ann stuck her thumb in the jam
and tasted it.

"But things like this don't happen,"
said Ben. "Except in stories."

"In stories about magic kingdoms, usually," said Ann. "It's quite good jam. Spell out BREAD."

Ben wrote BREAD in the sand.

The letters faded under the next wave.

Immediately thick slices of fresh bread appeared, on a golden tray.

Ann spelled out MILK, and waited.

And they had milk, in crystal goblets.

"You're right," said Ann. "It's more fun
to be in a story than to read one."

"It depends on the ending," said Ben.

"Most stories have happy endings," said Ann. "Can you spell BEACH UMBRELLA? The sun is hot."

Ben spelled TREE.

They ate in the shade of a young oak.
Ann spelled **CANDY**, for dessert.

"I still want a shell I can hear the sea in,"
said Ben. "Let's ask the king."

"What king?" said Ann. She offered the
box of candy to Ben.

"If this is a magic kingdom, there has
to be a king," said Ben.

"If you want a shell, you just have to spell it," said Ann. "You don't have to bother anybody."

But Ben had written KING in the sand.

A wave covered the letters.

"There he is," said Ann.

On a rock by the sea sat a king with a
fishing pole. He looked old and tired.

Ben and Ann walked over to him.

"It's a nice day, isn't it?" said Ben.

The king didn't look up. "Why have
you come here?" he said.

"To find a big shell," said Ben. "Are there any here in our kingdom?"

"Kingdom?" said the king.

"Did you catch any fish?" said Ann.

The king shook his head.

"You're a king," said Ben. "So
this must be a kingdom."

Ann's toe printed **FISH** in the sand.

"A kingdom is cities and farms," said
the king, "and forests and castles."

A fish flashed on the end of his line,
and he sat up straight to bring it in.

"Thank you for the bread and jam and things," said Ann.

"We had a nice picnic under the tree," said Ben.

The king turned and saw the oak at the edge of the sea. He let the fish swim free, and he put down the pole. Bent and limping, he walked slowly to the tree.

He looked up questioningly at the high
branches. He touched the sturdy trunk.

"This place was under a spell, I guess,"
said Ann. "And we broke it."

"Or is it under a spell now?" said the
 king. "Under your spell."

"Ours?" said Ann.

"We just spelled words," said Ben.

"Words with letters," said Ann.
"From the alphabet. Like this."

She spelled out FOREST.

"Of course," said the king.

He watched a wave wash out the letters. Then he turned and watched the tall trees spring up along the length of sandy beach.

"A royal forest," he said.

He seemed to grow taller, and younger.

Ben spelled out FARMS in the sand, Ann wrote CITIES, and the surf came in to wipe the words away.

Plowed farms appeared beyond the
trees, and meadows where cows grazed.

In the distance towns and cities
gleamed in the sun.

"It's a very pretty kingdom," said Ann.

"Hurry," said the king. "Castles."

Ben wrote CASTLES in big letters. They
were gone with the next swell of the sea.

Here and there castles rose above the
towns. And the kingdom was complete.

The king gazed at the faraway towers
of the tallest castle.

"I must get there in time," he said.

"Get where?" said Ben.

"To his throne, of course," said Ann.
"To all his knights, in shining armor."

From beneath his robe the king took a
large seashell, and he listened to it.

"It's a long journey," he said. "Even
on a fast charger."

He handed the shell to Ben. Ben
put it to his ear.

Ann spelled **HORSE** in the sand.

"I hear the sea," said Ben.

A charger stood on the edge of the
spit of sand. The king went to it with
long strides and hardly any limp.

"Farewell," he said.

"We'll ride with you," said Ben.

"No," said the king.

"Yes," said Ann. "We're in the story
too, aren't we?"

She and Ben ran along beside the horse through the woods. In a clearing the king drew on the reins and turned to face them.

His voice was stern.

"You must leave the kingdom," he said. "I command it. I am the king."

The charger reared and plunged into the forest, toward the castle.

Fading hoofbeats echoed in the trees.

"Go back to the beach and write PONY twice," said Ann. "We'll follow him."

Ben had the shell pressed to his ear.

"The king forgot his shell," said Ann.

"He meant to give it to me," said Ben.
"He knew it was what I came for."

He handed the shell to Ann.

"Yes, I know," she said. "You can hear the sea in it."

But she held the shell to her ear for a moment before she gave it back.

Suddenly she grabbed Ben's arm.

"I can still hear the sea," she said.

Ben stood listening. Without the shell
he heard the sea. It sounded close by.

He ran between the trees toward
the beach. Ann followed him.

A wave broke against the tree trunks,
splashing them.

"The tide is coming in," said Ben.

They ran in the direction of the hill,
through the forest near the edge
of the rising sea.

"Isn't there some part of the beach left?"
said Ann. "Where we can spell something?"

"Keep running," said Ben.

The water rose higher over the floor of
the forest with each breaking wave.

Through the trees they saw the high
hill of sand.

They panted, wading in the water
 above their knees.

"Hurry," said Ben.

"I am hurrying," said Ann.

With their last bit of breath they
climbed the steep hill of sand.

Behind it lay the solid high shore
and the cottage.

From the top of the hill they looked
down on the magic kingdom.

The tide was pouring in on the farms
and the green meadows.

It had risen high in the forest. Tops of trees were disappearing beneath it.

Towns and cities were sinking under the flood of blue water.

The tide rose higher and higher.

It covered the farms and the forests,
the towns and the cities.

Waves broke over the castles.

Soon only the tops of the castle towers
remained, glinting in the sun.

"I wonder if there was time," said Ann.

"Time for what?" said Ben.

"For a happy ending," said Ann.

"The tide came in too soon," said Ben.

The last castle tower had vanished. They gazed out across the unbroken sea.

Suddenly Ann stood up.

"The story didn't have any ending at all!"
she said. "When we left, it just stopped!"

She turned to Ben.

"The king is still there, in the story," she said. "Hoping to get to his throne."

But Ben had his ear to the shell, and he was listening to the sea.

Magic Beach, one of Crockett Johnson's most innovative books, nearly went unpublished because editors thought it too serious and difficult for children. Born David Johnson Leisk (rhymes with "disc") in 1906, Dave (as he was known to his friends) adopted the nickname Crockett as a child, later using Crockett Johnson as a pseudonym because, he explained, "Leisk was too hard to pronounce."[1] Though he gave himself a name that was easier to say, he never wrote down to his readers. Very bright and a voracious reader himself, Dave consistently created works that exceeded the limitations of the genre. His "Barnaby" (1942–52, 1960–62) was the epitome of the thinking person's comic strip. Its fans included Duke Ellington, W. C. Fields, Charles Schulz, and Dorothy Parker, who called it "the most important addition to American arts and letters in Lord knows how many years."[2] His seven-book *Harold and the Purple Crayon* series (1955–63) not only won the admiration of award-winning illustrators Maurice Sendak and William Joyce, but Chris Van Allsburg actually thanked "Harold, and his purple crayon" in the acceptance speech for his first Caldecott Medal. Former U.S. Poet Laureate Rita Dove names *Harold* as her first favorite book because "it showed me the possibilities of traveling on the line of one's imagination.... That made a powerful impression on me."[3]

In 1958, after Dave had written his first four books about Harold's purple crayon and one book about Ellen's lion, Ursula Nordstrom—his editor at Harper and Brothers—asked if he'd be interested in writing a *Harold* story for Harper's "I Can Read" series. These books, inaugurated by Else Holmelund Minarik's *Little Bear* (illustrated by Sendak) in 1957, were intended for beginning readers: Dave would need to write at a slightly lower reading level than he had for his other *Harold* tales. Dave said he would be interested. So, after writing *Harold's Circus* (1959), he began work on a *Harold* "I Can Read" book. Inspired by the legend of the Fisher King, Dave found himself writing not about Harold but about loss and imagination in what would be his most beautiful, poetic, and abstract story yet: *Magic Beach*.

When he sent the manuscript of *Magic Beach* to Ursula in early April of 1959, he acknowledged the Fisher King influence, adding, "I am happy to say that I have avoided adding to the confusion by making sociological analogies as [T. S.] Eliot did." He continued, with typically dry wit:

> I believe I have restored to the legend some of its pre-Christian purity by making the grail a mollusk shell. You will notice I have used no part of Mallory's or de Troyes' cloak and dagger crap. Perceval (or Parsifal) becomes in this version a couple of typical American kids and the wasteland is nothing but an ordinary old sandbar. I am just telling you all this in case you happen to publish the book and somebody writes in, say a librarian, asking what it is supposed to be about. It is a variation on a poetic theme, a lesson in physical geography, a Safety council message, and a spelling bee, all rolled into one.

Though he added what he half-mockingly called an "'I Can Spell' gimmick" to the tale (in having the children spell out words on the beach), Dave noted that unless books in the "I Can Read" series "have made considerable headway in stamping out illiteracy in the age group, this is not an 'I Can Read' book." While confident of the quality of his story, he wondered if his illustrations would work: "These doubts have to do with the limitations of my style where a convincing realism and use of perspective is called for by the text." He worried that the spelling device might remind people too much of Harold, and noted that in *Harold's Fairy Tale* (1956), "I touched on the wasteland and a fisher king (albeit sans flyrod)."[4]

In the reader's report for Harper and Brothers, Susan Carr (later Hirschman) wrote, "It misses all around. It is not funny, it is not serious, and it is not a lovely combination of the two.... I truly do not see any way to rewrite this story to make it successful." In conclusion, Susan observed, "This is no book with which to follow up *Ellen's Lion* [1959]. It is almost impossible to believe they are written by the same man."[5] Ursula called Dave later in April to break the news to him more gently. He conceded, "I know it is the kind of thing that has to hit somebody just right or it must go as a miss entirely." He asked her to send *Magic Beach* back, and she did.[6]

Dave then wrote an "I Can Read" book about Harold, *A Picture for Harold's Room*, which Ursula liked so much that she featured it on the cover of Harper and Brothers' spring 1960 catalogue. After a successful television production of "Barnaby and Mr. O'Malley" (starring Ron Howard and Bert Lahr in the title roles), Dave revived his "Barnaby" strip and began work on a second book about Ellen and her lion. By April of 1962, however, the new "Barnaby" had ended its run, and Dave put Ellen aside so that he could return once again to *Magic Beach*. After rewriting and shortening it, he decided it was "much better than the old one," and sent the manuscript back to Ursula.[7] Ann Jorgensen (now Tobias), the reader at Harper (which had by then become Harper & Row), thought the story too "depressing" and complex for children.[8] Ursula herself admitted, "As an adult I love the mood of the story, and the tone of sadness. But we're afraid that it just isn't a children's book."[9] So, Dave finished his new *Ellen* book, and wrote his seventh and last *Harold* book, *Harold's ABC*. But he did not give up on *Magic Beach*. Considering it "far and away the best small thing I have done," he sent it to half a dozen other publishers, all of whom "enthusiastically... turned down" the book.[10]

A couple of years later, Holt, Rinehart and Winston accepted the manuscript but not the illustrations. Perhaps feeling that such an abstract story needed more concrete pictures, Holt contacted Estelle and Betty Mandel, the agents of Betty Fraser, a young freelance illustrator whose work had appeared in trade and fashion magazines. She was very surprised to be chosen: after all, Crockett Johnson was already a well-known illustrator and her style was so different from his. However, she pushed her doubts aside and took the job. Looking back on it now, Betty seems almost embarrassed by her work. When told that Dave considered this one of his best books, Betty (who never met him) said, "Oh, Lord, I can imagine what he had to say about my illustrations."[11] So, with elaborate illustrations very unlike Dave's own, *Magic Beach* was published as *Castles in the Sand* in

1965. Reviewers were not as baffled as the readers at Harper & Row, but they did wonder what children would make of it. *The New York Times Book Review*'s Barbara Novak O'Doherty admitted that the book was "perhaps a little too oblique for a child," but nonetheless felt that Crockett Johnson "lifts the standard in children's literature considerably with this attempt, and I'm all for it."[12]

So am I. *Magic Beach* offers Crockett Johnson's most developed examination of the boundary between real and imaginary worlds, a prominent theme in "Barnaby," the *Harold* books, and the *Ellen* books. It is not so much a departure from his earlier work as it is a more finely tuned, carefully nuanced exploration of his favorite theme: the powers and limits of the imagination. For the first time, readers can find *Magic Beach* as Crockett Johnson intended it—and the first "new" work written and illustrated by Johnson since 1965.

Following the three children's books he published in 1965, Johnson left the children's book business altogether, returning only to illustrate *The Happy Egg* (1967) by his wife, Ruth Krauss. In November of 1965, he started a new career as an artist and amateur mathematician, beginning a series of paintings inspired by famous theorems. In all, he painted about one hundred large, vivid canvases of geometric shapes that are visually kin to the "color field" abstract expressionist paintings of Mark Rothko, Ad Reinhardt, and Barnett Newman. He also published two original mathematical theorems.

In early February of 1975, Dave—a lifelong smoker—learned that he had lung cancer. At first he thought that a skilled surgeon might be able to remove the cancer. When author Doris Lund saw him a few weeks after the diagnosis, she asked, "How are you doing, Dave?" He replied sardonically, "They're all rushing around, looking for the fastest switchblade in the West."[13] But the cancer proved inoperable. On July 11, 1975, he died at the age of 68.

Concluding the long (and somewhat tongue-in-cheek) explanation that he sent to Ursula Nordstrom back in 1959, Johnson wrote, "But enough with tedious prefaces. Sit back and enjoy the story."[14] To echo his words, enough with this afterword. Turn to the beginning, then sit back and enjoy the story.

NOTES

[1] Lee Bennett Hopkins, *Books Are by People: Interviews with 104 Authors and Illustrators of Books for Young Children* (New York: Citation Press, 1969), 124.

[2] Dorothy Parker, "A Mash Note to Crockett Johnson," *PM*, 3 October 1943, 16.

[3] Chris Van Allsburg, "1982 Caldecott Medal Acceptance"; Rita Dove, in *For the Love of Books*, ed. Ronald B. Shwartz (New York: Grosset/Putnam, 1999), 32.

[4] Crockett Johnson, letter to Ursula Nordstrom, 7 April 1959.

[5] Susan Carr, reader's report on *Magic Beach*, Harper and Brothers, 8 April 1959.

[6] Johnson, postcard to Ursula Nordstrom, 28 April 1959.

[7] Johnson, postcard to Ursula Nordstrom, n.d. [c. 7 May 1962].

[8] Ann Jorgensen, reader's report on *Magic Beach*, Harper & Row, 8 May 1962.

[9] Ursula Nordstrom, letter to Johnson, 9 May 1962.

[10] Johnson, letter to Ursula Nordstrom, 12 December 1962.

[11] Betty Fraser, interview with Philip Nel, 12 June 2000.

[12] Barbara Novak O'Doherty, "The World of Tangerine Cats and Cabbage Moons," *New York Times Book Review*, 9 May 1965, 4.

[13] Doris Lund, interview with Philip Nel, 20 June 2000.

[14] Johnson, letter to Ursula Nordstrom, 7 April 1959.